Mystic Lands

The Sympathy Dragon and the Prejudice King

Book One

LEON LOWE

To order additional copies of this book, contact:
Xlibris
UK TFN: 0800 0148620 (Toll Free inside the UK)
UK Local: 02 0369 56328 (+44 20 3695 6328 from outside the UK)
www.xlibrispublishing.co.uk
Orders@ Xlibrispublishing.co.uk

ISBN: Softcover   978-1-6641-1794-5
         EBook   978-1-6641-1795-2

Print information available on the last page

Rev. date: 06/22/2022

Mystic Lands

CHAPTER 1

There Once Lived a King

Once there lived a Dragon in a mystical Kingdom full of Knights and Wizards. This Dragon was special and had a heart of sympathy, love and fairness.

There were many dragons in the Kingdom with special abilities but this one was different.

This Dragon was the most special. This was a Dragon who had power over the elements and authority over kinship and sustenance.

When it rained from the clouds the Sympathy Dragon had the power to turn droplets of the rain extra clean and by turning the droplets extra clean the land would become fertile.

In this Kingdom was a Castle and in this Castle lived a King who ruled over 13 noble houses including his own. Every Morning the Dragon would fly over the Castle and his wingspan would freshen the atmosphere.

The king's Castle full of its knights, maidens, lords and ladies had a particular Knight who was dedicated with a heart of justice to the royal chivalry system.

In this royal chivalry system, knights were given powers as stewards to look over the ward of an estate, village, town, town district, county district, county, the city district, city, region, country, or Kingdom.

The knights and maidens were given power under the lord stewards and regents. The knights and maidens had charge over the estates, villages, towns and town districts.

The Lord stewards were given power and charge over county districts, county, and city districts, and city and the royal regents were given power over regions and the country.

The main royal/noble house where the king lived with his queen was and had power, authority, ward and charge throughout the whole Kingdom.

In this Kingdom there dwelt many magical creatures who the kings and queens as well as the royal and noble houses had dominion over.

Fairies were renowned for their good magic and wondrous splendour.

The magic of fairies was similar to the magic of nature deities the very magic beings that fairies descend from. Witches were famed for their principled magic and marvellous cooking.

Wizards were known for making wonderful medicines and helping the ill.

Royal kings and queens were in place in the 13 households of the land tasked with upkeep and oversight of all goings-on and governing of the Kingdom and the people in it.

Mythical magical amazing Birds. Flew through the land and commanded by the Dragon they cleaned and curated the ecosystem of the land.

In the queen's Castle lived six queen Maidens and the Queen of benevolence who was married to the prejudice king unhappily of course.

The queen's four maidens all had a duty and so their title spoke of them.

The maiden of the hunt, the maiden of sport, the maiden of potions, the maiden of spells.

They are the queens, four maidens of the estate and ladies of the land.

The sympathy dragon would subdue the land daily and with as much work ethic for to subdue is to give time and effort in the form of talents.

CHAPTER 2

The Prejudice King

One day a decree goes out in the land by the Prejudice King.

King Pedro who earned the title of the prejudice king one day awoke in his room to the flapping of wings and a change of scent in the air.

He awoke alone to a splendidly luxurious but on second inspection it seemed quite messy.

There was spaghetti and meatballs in a big pot by his side and it had begun to grow fungus from the night before.

He calls in one of his servants.

King Pedro, "Butler! Butler"! He calls out in a coarse tone, and his butler comes running in.

Butler "Yes, sire". the butler says to the King. The King turns to the butler and says. "What is making that terrible racket and why is there that smell"?

The butler, "It is the dragon who rules the land, he makes that smell every morning. It is what he does".

King Pedro, "Clean up this mess and alert my lords to a town hall assembly meeting. We have to discuss this infernal racket and terrible stench".

That very evening the Prejudice King meets his lords in the meeting room we come to know as the grand hall. Many noble lords and ladies arrive and seat themselves.

The Queen Maiden who is the wife of the Prejudice King sits next to the Prejudice King, King Pedro. The Prejudice King turns and says to her, King Pedro, My lady, I am so glad you could make it".

The Queen maiden turns to King Pedro and says.

Queen maiden, "I am only here because I am the only one in the land powerful enough to stop you. This does not change things between us".

King Pedro goes to stand at the plinth and begins to speak. King Pedro orders that all dragons must be taken away and destroyed. He sits in his chair and continues to speak. "My lords and ladies I have brought you all here today for one reason and one reason only and that is to inform you that I am partitioning for the destruction and exile of every dragon in the land. Understand that all noble houses have attended and are seated in the dining area. Please would everyone with an envelope and pen and that is everyone please vote claiming yay or nay to the destruction and exile of dragons from the land".

All who are in attendance vote and a law is passed. The King soon seeks to destroy and exile like a bigot all the dragons from the land. He sets up a regal challenge to find an exceptional troop of knights to diminish the values that the good dragons in the land stood for and take away their rightful homes. He stands in his courts at a time of full house and tells his peers and subjects.

CHAPTER 3

The Seven Knights

King Pedro, "The time has come for you to serve your King", all knights and lords in this court must battle for the affections of the King. Show me who is the mightiest of warriors in a tournament of challenges and I will regard you as a Knight and Steward of great note, deed and title".

The crowd cheer and then the tournaments begin. Jousting is the first tournament and half are relegated to lower ranks

Sword fighting is the second tournament and a quarter are given middle ranks.

Running and best times assume the highest ranks; the fastest time is for the chief general and the slowest time is for the lance corporal. There is just one challenge left to decide the rank of the last seven.

Out of the regal challenges come the tournaments and at these tournaments, there are seven contenders and unknown to them each one of the seven is now part of the troop but they don't know that as yet. They all get summoned to the king's castle to be briefed on their first mission, a mission which will decide their ranks and just exactly who is the leader. Unbeknown to the knights the King has rebelled against nature and instead of capturing a dragon they just maybe there to destroy it.

King Pedro "This is your final test to bring in the dragon. Whosoever has the best score is the leader of the seven chief generals and will behold the title of steward of knights, the rest of you will be deputies and assigned tasks under the steward. We will be looking at power, skill, competence, strength and ability".

Antony Valour, "Yes, sir I will not fail you as the highest-scoring contender in each contest I will ensure honour is brought to your name and that my service is one of justice".

King Pedro "I am relying on your service. Do well by me and you will be richly rewarded". The seven knights cheer!

On their first mission, they meet with an Elf who is guarding the Sympathy Dragon at his forest retreat. At the forest retreat, it appears the King has become deceptive with scrolls. The elf has on him at his address and on his person scrolls detailing rewards for the caretakers of dragons in the forms of grants and care packages.

CHAPTER 4

The Sympathy Dragon

The seven knights come wandering into the dwelling place of the Guardian Elf.

Antony valour, "I am here on orders of the King".

The Caretaker Elf who is guarding the Sympathy Dragon runs out of a tree stump and says.

Caretaker Elf, "Are you here to give me my reward and much-needed trinkets for the upkeep of the sympathy dragon and his services to the kingdom".

The Elf explains how he was given the summons to get tools for his rest bite so he could maintain the energy to look after his dragon.

Anthony valour, "No, we are here to collect the dragon, where is it"?

Caretaker Elf, "I guess that's so I can have a rest from my caretaker duties and refresh. Come this way I will show you where I am keeping the Sympathy Dragon safe and protected".

Evil Knight 1, "Exactly that, now show us where the Sympathy Dragon is so we can take him in".

The Elf shows an empty doubtful expression but haste and desperateness lead them through the rich citadel. The citadel has a rich array of edifice buildings, a tower with plenty of cream grey and stone luxury marble, a golden temple where the sympathy dragon is and a lovely cottage where the keys to the temple of the sympathy dragon are. Believing the best and also perceiving that he is receiving an appraisal the elf shows them to his cottage in the forest. They walk through an area of trees until they arrive at a forest of bushes and overhanging plants.

Behind that space is a small citadel for the dragon and elf.

A cottage and a castle cave are the two buildings that lead onto the golden temple where the Sympathy Dragon resides. The exit at the back of the cottage.

The Elf says the magic words "arb"! Then the 8 people enter what appears to be a cave in a castle.

The Elf taps his hands three times on a magic panel and soon two keys are revealed.

The Elf takes the key saying to the Knights. "This is the key that unlocks the obedient wait of the Sympathy Dragon. These keys have mystical qualities as they were breathed into existence by the Sympathy Dragon as a testament to his obedience to the land and kingdom". They make their way through the castle until they come to the centre where there appears to be a golden temple about half the size of the castle cave.

"We're here". Says the Elf and then he uses one of the keys to enter the temple. Soon the Knights show him their true colours and begin to raid the place.

Evil knight 1, "Show us where the Sympathy Dragon lurks and we will spare your life".

Antony Valour turns to them sparingly and says with a tone of subtle hope and innocent confusion.

Anthony Valour, "Is this man wanted for a crime? We are as he said here to collect a dragon for the king's agenda.

Evil knight 2, "And that we will do".

The evil knights talk to each other about Antony's Valour. Antony goes with the Elf and finds that Sympathy Dragon we will take care of what he said in here.

Antony Valour, Can you assure me you will take care of this elf's needs? You will protect his virtue and nurture his quill with benevolence. Quill means to ensure due diligence and the utmost benevolence. For the good knight to mention these words indicated he was the well-meaning friend of the elf.

Evil knight 3, "You have our word".

Antony Valour "Knights honour".

Evil knights exclaim, "Knights honour"!

The Elf and the Good Knight enter the sympathy dragon's temple. And approach the Dragon. The elf holds out his key and goes to unlock the sympathy dragon's chain of obedience. The sympathy dragon speaks in telephony towards the Guardian Elf.

CHAPTER 5

The Sympathy Dragons Temple

Sympathy Dragon, "What are you doing here today elf and why are you unbinding me"?

Guardian Elf, "This man is going to provide you benevolent care in the palace of the king of the land".

Sympathy Dragon "Wait, I sense a strange confusion in him, a confusion that could bring me danger and blight, he may not be taking me to the care of a good king but instead a Prejudice swindler. You must not let me go with him".

He screams and hollers but no one cares. The dragon is then led away and peacefully walks alongside the knights' although twenty times his size. The six evil knights show Antony a wanted poster of the dragon and the elf.

Evil knight 4, One of the knights, the good knight turns to him and says, "I have to take you away to the dungeon at King Pedro's castle for questioning".

The elf asks why and the knight tells him, "you have been harbouring a criminal". The knights tie him up and lead him to the castle. At the castle, the Prejudice King orders the elf's execution but the good knight tricks the Prejudice King Pedro into allowing him to do it. The good knight takes the elf out of the castle and draws his sword. He goes to swing it and the appearance of blood appears everywhere although we do not get a clear angle from the castle of the elf's death. The Good Knight gives the Elf directions to his tavern in the woods and tells him you will be safe there until I figure out what all of this is for. He puts the Elf on horseback, unties him and whispers to his Horse. The Horse and Elf ride away on towards the Good Knight rest bite tavern. The Good Knight makes his way back to the castle.

Back in the castle. King Pedro or the Prejudice King as he will soon be known gets his royal guard to choose a knight to slay a particular dragon. He requests one that is brave, strong and hates Dragons. The Knights Guard chose Anthony Valour as the most up and coming knight overall. Anthony Valour asks the King whether his Quest is one of honour Justice love and mercy.

The king tells him he is determined to rid the world of cruel and ugly dragons and that he is bound by decree and shouldn't argue with his ruler. The Prejudice King tells him he must honour his Duty before the Prestigious majesty of the King, the rightful ruler of the Land.

One of the lords whispers to the king. "Antony Valour was the only knight in your kingdom not in attendance"!

CHAPTER 6

Prejudice is a Disservice to the Just

King Pedro, "You have done my bidding and out of all of the knights that were sent to the Sympathy Dragon you were the one who captured the Dragon. For your grand victory you will become my Lord of knights and from here go out seeking all dragons of the land so they can be brought to me and trained to be beasts of my kingdom and learn to cultivate my culture and traditions and kinship of mine king Pedro's kingdom". Anthony Valour, the good knight agrees and tells the Predijuice King "I am honoured and privileged. It is my duty by honour, decree and privilege to serve in your courts and I will do so".

The king tells him to get some rest. "rest tomorrow afternoon you bring me another dragon. I expect to see you back here to bring in another Dragon after that and then another and another and another until all the dragons are mine.

Across the kingdom, at the tavern, the one the Good Knight and Humble Wizard own together as cousins in a business partnership and as a noble household, a maiden from over the wood is eating lunch when an Elf on horseback arrives and falls through a window she had just opened. The Maiden and the Humble Wizard attend him and he tells them everything.

Anthony goes back to his home on horseback and arrives at the tavern where he is greeted by his friend the Humble Wizard who also bartends and runs an eating clinic.

The knight wanders into the tavern they own together as joint aires of a noble household. In the tavern, a maiden sits and eats peaceably.

The Wizard works and he also part-owns and tells the Good Knight all that happened to the artisan Elf. The Good Knight lets them know of his good and pure intentions to serve with goodness and honour.

Artie the Guardian Elf, "He was there, this is one of the knights who kidnapped the Dragon".

Morris the Humble wizard. "No Antony wouldn't be this dishonourable. What happened".

Antony the Good Knight "It's the Predijuce King Pedro".

Scarlett the maiden "What do you mean by the Predijuce king Pedro? I thought it was just King Pedro".

Antony the Good Knight "It seems as though King Pedro has developed an evil attitude, one of bias opinions and slanderous actions". Artie the elf "Explain"!

Antony the good knight, "When I signed up to be a high ranking official of the King's court I was expecting justice and honour, goodness and mercy. Just recently I have come to realise that king Pedro and his current officials are none of those things. He is quite the opposite every day a new decree goes out more wicked and merciless than the one before a stone of insecurity lives in the court and is spoken by the predijuce king".

Scarlett the maiden, "How is the dragon? What did you do with him"?

Antony the Good Knight, When my time with King Pedro was over, instead of slaying the dragon I took him away to the place where I first found him with the key Artie gave me.

Artie the elf, "So what are you saying".

Antony the good knight, "I am saying the dragon is perfectly safe in the place where he began".

Morris the humble wizard, "Saddle up, we make camp there tonight".

The four heroes make their way to the elf's secret woodland retreat and enter the temple where the Sympathy Dragon is.

CHAPTER 7

The Kindness of Strangers

Sympathy Dragon, "Artie and his friends, the kind and noble Antony thank you for your help".

Artie, "Sympathy Dragon I apologise for my disbelief it seems as though the King has rebelled against the land and its protector".

Sympathy Dragon, "The fate of the King rests on his morals and the nature of his character.

All we can do is hope and pray that days change for the better. True royalty is grace and honours noble and merciful the Predijuce King will soon learn this".

The next day a decree goes out to the land to slay all dragons that live in the land none are individually targeted this time but all are exterminated instead. A Knight, a Wizard and a Maiden along with an Artisan Elf set up a guild to protect the Sympathy Dragon. They hide the Sympathy Dragon in a mystical temple where the Sympathy Dragon grants powers to the four heroes to take care of the Sympathy Dragon.

Suddenly in the sympathy dragon's temple, a flaming ember appears and a spirit of light is evoked, it's the nature deity.

Nature deity, "Sympathy dragon it is me the nature deity of this land and I am here to tell the spirits from beyond have deemed the bias king his courts and all in the land unworthy. For his bias ways and dishonour to the kingdom, we have decided to set a famine on the land, a famine that only you can remedy. Thank you sympathy dragon and remember love is kind and the truth will set you free".

The Wizard is given the ability of magical insight and is endowed with a new golden staff, the Good Knight is given the ability of strength and remarkable power, and the Elf is given the ability of a quick and wondrous mind and the ability to be a marvellous hunter. The Maiden is given the ability to see visions and also is given the ability to create pills, potions and the ability to heal.

The Sympathy Dragon is granted magical powers of protection and safety by the Nature Deity and a seal is cast over the temple cave. Only those who truly love and care for the Sympathy Dragon can access a vision of the temple. In this temple is a grand palace where the Good Knight, Humble Wizard, Guardian Elf, Sympathy Dragon and Gentle Maiden all live in peaceful bliss and harmony.

The Nature Deity did this because of purpose. The Sympathy Dragon had a purpose, and the King had a purpose but the King had betrayed the Sympathy Dragon and perverted his purpose by not adhering to the needs of the Dragon and believing in him and his purpose.

Now the potent purpose of the Sympathy Dragon was to keep the grounds fertile and the people peaceful. Cleanliness, helpfulness, nurturing and health endorsing the sympathy made sure all people of the land were well-groomed and maintained.

Seven days after the Predijuce king banished the Sympathy Dragon, drought and famine fell on the land. This was the longest and most severe drought and famine the mystic lands had ever known. This would be the last seven days of King Pedro's mortal reign.

On the first day of the drought, the courtyards and the King starved. On the second day of the drought, all of King Pedro's men lost their energy and were unable to work for him. On the third day of the drought and famine, there was a noble partition declaring six feudal houses of the land defunct from the king. On the fourth day of the drought. All the nobles of the land began to drink a strange slime which made them sick. On the fifth day of the drought and famine, all of King Pedro's noble followers became ogre-like creatures and on the sixth day of the drought and famine King, Pedro made a deal with the Nature Deity to restore his kingdom unbeknown to him the Nature Deity was the wife of the Sympathy Dragon.

CHAPTER 8

The Nature Deity's Blessing

Nature Deity, "On one condition".

King Pedro, "What's that"!

Nature Deity, "You abandon the swine who tried to swindle my husband".

King Pedro, "You have my word Nature Deity. Consider the swine cursed".

On the seventh day when King Pedro arose to sit at his chair in his grand palace, he was greeted by ogres. All of them were smelly and wouldn't go away.

He told them to do his bidding and that they were bound by the decree. Of course, they all agreed in hysteria and confusion they listened with an attitude to the King.

The King told them that they must return his lords and ladies but they nobly reminded the King that they are his lords and ladies.

The King said he didn't believe them and that they are all liars and that for lying to him they'll pay the price but they just laughed and wandered off saying oh what a scoff.

One hour had passed and fatigue set in. hunger, thirst and the vileness within.

Soon his Predijuce, this Predijuce of a King would be a burden and become the heavyweight of not listening.

His skin began to burn and turn thin to the bone but it was not rubble that sat on this throne. Just bones and garments on the chairs where they stay. The Predijuce king had lived his last day.

Prejudice King, "You will follow my lead. You are my ogres now".

Evil ogre lord, "And you are our demon troll".

Prejudice King, "You're demon troll has something to tell you. Listen to me and me alone".

Evil ogre lord, "What is it?"

Prejudice King, "To restore ourselves we must find that Sympathy Dragon".

Evil ogre lord, "But isn't that what got us into this mess in the first place".

Prejudice King, "Listen if you were smarter than me they would have made you King and not me".

Evil ogre lord, "Let's hear it".

Prejudice King, "That Nature Deity has something to do with the Sympathy Dragon. Find the Sympathy Dragon we find the Nature Deity then get her to reverse all of this".

Evil ogre lord, "I'll tell the team".

Prejudice king, "And whilst you're out try and find some food".

The Prejudice King in his reckless ordinance sends out scouting parties in the form of ogre knights and ogre lords to find food for each knight troupe led by a cunning lord of the king's court.

During one of the missions, the good knight is called into duty and investigates the goings-on of the king's court after a week of famine. After the mission and no food is found the good knight reports back to the sympathy dragon.

The good knight explains he was on a consort mission for food when his troupe began to eat each other because of hunger.

The wizard tells the sympathy dragon he was looking for some edible herb for his potion to cultivate the land.

The two champions among the seven maidens ask the sympathy dragon for her help.

They explain famine at the castle and the wizard explains drought and famine at his cove. The sympathy dragon gets them to promise to not tell the king or anyone outside of the temple his whereabouts; they promise to keep his word.

Back at the castle when king Pedro the bias king discovers that the good knight has not been attending duties he makes him a fugitive and orders a decree through the land to find and arrest the good knight.

The good knight sees his picture go on a post and the post reads most wanted the good knight of the mystic lands wanted for disobeying the king.

The good knight reports back to the sympathy dragon and the sympathy dragon agree to take extra care of the needs of the good knight.

The humble wizard tells the sympathy dragon a few noble households have kept the dragon's ways in the mystic lands and have not given into bias and mercilessness becoming cannibals and hunting for innocent magic creatures.

CHAPTER 9

The Shame of Disobedience

The sympathy dragon looks upon them with obedient mercy and a tear drops from his eyes into a medication dispenser to be used later for magic spells. The dragon begins to tell them, "now good knight and humble wizard". Take this tear to the other side of the land away from the bias king and find some soil. Pour the droplet onto the soul, go into the humble wizard's castle cove and leave it there overnight, recite this prayer and sleep afterwards. Dragon of sympathy free the mystic lands, thank you for your obedience, patience and benevolence towards us, we praise your tenacity in the morning when you awake food will be there for you but do not share it.

The humble wizard and the good knight journey through the land until they come to the humble wizard's castle cove. They do exactly as the sympathy dragon says and the next morning they have food for the next year. They gather it all up and take it to the sympathy dragon's temple cave.

The year passes and soon they find that the bias king has died of malnutrition. In his castle a demonic magic reigns and even though his proof, skin and eyes have passed from him he still speaks moves and commands his overlord troupe of ogres who have now become sub-human mutants.

In his place, the lords and ladies system has taken over but they are just as idols as the bias king. The lords and ladies have all become tall obese ogres whereas the bias king has become their magic control and every command. The ogres become so used to the bias king's instruction that they only listen to his every welp and sad pathetic look. When you look at the Prejudice king long enough you can start to become controlled by his evil powerful control and abuse of authority.

When the patrons, also the lords and ladies who are cannibals, begin to suspect that their high-class cannibal system has not gone everywhere they investigate their fugitive knight,

Ogre lord "the good knight. Sure does have a lot of explaining to do". Ogre lady "he certainly does". He was the most favoured knight in the courts of king Pedro".

Ogre lord "I'll send out a troupe of knights to arrest him in his castle. We should find him this time".

Ogre lady "send only lords this time you might find him that way".

Ogre lord "if the bias king could see him know he would be turning in his throne".

Ogre lady "when you get there check if they are ogres".

The ogre rallies a troupe of ogre lords and tells them

Ogre lord "right ogre lords we have a mission to fulfil our best knight has got to make the upgrade".

Ogre lord 2 "but isn't he a fugitive". Ogre lord "that was last year, this year were ogres. We need to find him and bring him in along with that wizard he's been spotted with, that way we can get help".

Ogre 3 "what do we need help for were ogres". All the ogres cheer.

Ogre Lord, Well, he is a fugitive and we got to find him anyway so come with me". All the ogres cheer and walk off exiting the castle grounds.

CHAPTER 10

March of the Ogre Lords

The ogre lords search day and knight in every corner of the kingdom until one day. The humble wizard and the good knight make their errands through the noble lands carrying food parcels on mules and horseback around the noble houses unaffected by the famine.

Humble wizard "that was the last food parcel we can return to the palace".

Good knight, "Let us just do that".

Soon enough after their last errand, they come across a troupe of evil ogre lords. The ogre lords watch their last delivery and overhear them.

Ogre lord "you what, your last delivery".

Ogre lord 1, "you're supposed to be eating people not extinct food". The ogre lords begin to show the good knight and the humble wizard they should not be becoming ogres with a violent attack.

Humble wizard "I shouldn't have opened my big mouth now they will be looking for us".

Good knight "we must stay and fight for the trust of the innocent and the safety of what's good and pure will be troubled and endangered". The knight draws his sword and the wizard swings his staff. Soon the knight and the wizard overpower the four evil ogre lords and then begin to question them.

And they explain that since the bias king ordered all dragons exiled the natural ecosystem of the land has been out of flux.

They then tell them if they find out you have been hiding a dragon we will report you to the king.

The Prejudice king is dead in breath tone, skin, flesh and brain matter but his evil spirit still sits on the throne with his voice whispering to his followers telling them to be faithless and cruel about things that are not yet understood or well taken to. The evil lords after a year of pillaging and thuggery see that the good knight and the humble wizard have not been interacting and that their search parties keep getting lost. They conspire to seek and destroy the wizard and the knight for their practising and dedication to goodness and humility. Back at the Prejudice kings courts.

The evil lords employ an evil sorcerer to find where the wizard and the knight are hiding. They use a water bowl and crystals to find the location of the good knight and the humble wizard.

Evil ogre lord, "We've found them they are in the phoenix lands approaching the territories that have not yet accepted the bias king's demands"

Evil ogre lord 2, "We must send out all or as much of as we can to turn the remaining kingdoms of the mystic lands into ogres"

Evil ogre lord 3, "I'll get all the ogres that are still in the courts to attend the last six kingdoms and any ogre we see on the way can come with us and all"

In the temple of the sympathy, dragons are seven maidens and an eighth priestess maiden who is the leader and high priestess of the seven maidens. We could call them the high priestess maiden and the seven maidens. The high priestess maiden's name is veronica.

The seven maidens are duty-bound followers of the high priestess who endeavours to teach the maidens etiquette and decency.

The seven maidens in the temple with the sympathy dragon follow the laws of goodness, humility and sympathy as they tend to their daily tasks. They wake in the morning, clean their bodies, cook for each other, wash and clean the temple dwelling then edify and enrich the sympathy dragon on what they had learnt the previous day.

CHAPTER 11

Final Days of the Mystic Land, Battle Approaches

On one of these days, the sympathy dragon discovers a plot to find the good knight and the humble wizard through a dream vision he had.

The seer and the witch "two of the leading maidens of the seven maidens" tell the sympathy dragon his sympathetic deed to the land is finally being unravelled and the last of the good nobles are being hunted. All because the good knight and humble wizard resisted the proud bias of the evil and prejudice of King Pedro.

The evil lords begin to mark 12 territories that have not conceded to cannibalism and thuggery. The sear tells them that the evil lords have found all 12 noble territories still under the sympathy dragon's reign whilst looking through the psychic waters of a water basin.

The maidens with the sympathy dragon in his hidden temple cook clean and attend to duties. The maiden sear brings the sympathy dragon water and begins to clean him she tells him of a vision she had in the vision bowl.

Priestess maiden, "I have discovered a plot in the water bowl and I communed with the crystal ball also".

Sympathy dragon, "What did you find"?

Priestess maiden, "Your sympathetic deeds have begun to unravel. The evil lords are due to discover the community in the dragon kingdom who had not betrayed the spirit deity of nature "for cannibalism" and soon they will find us".

Sympathy dragon, "Which community are they going to"?

Priestess maiden, "I saw two crests belonging to four regents. One from each of the six remaining lands. First being the house of the phoenix, second being the house of the cat. The other houses have all given in to the law of the land third being the house of the squirrel, the fourth being the house of the dragon, the fifth being the house of the bear and the sixth being the house of the lizard. all of these houses still serve you but four of them have been discovered by the evil lords and conquered. We must send word to the other two. By doing this we may be able to overcome the invading hordes of evil lords before their corruption settles in."

Sympathy dragon, "Notify Antony and Aaron! I will need their expertise as a qualified knight and excellent wizard to go on an expedition through the last two kingdoms to warn and hopefully rescue them from impending corruption and doom from the evil lords".

The priestess maiden sets out of the sympathy dragon's temple with a scroll intent on finding the wizard and the knight to let them know about the two noble houses of the phoenix and the dragon. Antony the good knight and Aaron teller the humble wizard continue their journey through the once rich kingdoms of the mystic lands.

Everywhere they go they pass either someone enslaved to cannibals or an ogre feeding on what was once a rich human being. They come to an abandoned place where they camp overnight in an abandoned temple in the squirrel lands. Veronica the high priestess continues her journey through the night on a horseback riding like the wind. She uses a magical compass to track the whereabouts of her two gilded friends Antony and Aaron.

Soon enough she comes into confrontation with a pack of ogres and cannibals. They follow behind her, what appears to be twenty of them. Veronica arrives at the abandoned temple at the top of the morning followed by a horde of twenty ogres. She runs into the temple and wakes up Aaron and Antony. The two men soon fend off the horde of invading ogres with Aaron's magical staff and Antony's fighting stance.

When the horde is defeated Veronica turns to the two and says.

Veronica priestess maiden, "Quickly follow me to the phoenix land and then the dragon lands there are still two kingdoms that are unaffected by the evil spirit of the Prejudice king".

The three gilded friends get on horseback and ride like the wind until they reach the phoenix lands.

THE END.

T.B.C

Lightning Source UK Ltd.
Milton Keynes UK
UKHW050611100722
405605UK00002B/72